RUBY THE RED FAIRY
1-84362-016-2

AMBER THE ORANGE FAIRY
1-84362-017-0

SAFFRON THE YELLOW FAIRY
1-84362-018-9

FERN THE GREEN FAIRY
1-84362-019-7

SKY THE BLUE FAIRY
1-84362-020-0

INKY THE INDIGO FAIRY
1-84362-021-9

HEATHER THE VIOLET FAIRY
1-84362-022-7

Collect all seven Rainbow Magic
books to bring the sparkle
back to Fairyland...

Dedicated to Joanna Pilkington,
who found fairies in her
beautiful garden

Special thanks to
Narinder Dhami

ORCHARD BOOKS
96 Leonard Street, London EC2A 4XD
Orchard Books Australia
32/45-51 Huntley Street, Alexandria, NSW 2015
A Paperback Original
First published in Great Britain in 2003
Text © Working Partners Limited 2003
Created by Working Partners Limited, London W6 0QT
Illustrations © Georgie Ripper 2003
The right of Georgie Ripper to be identified as the illustrator
of this work has been asserted by her in accordance
with the Copyright, Designs and Patents Act, 1988.
A CIP catalogue record for this book is available
from the British Library.
ISBN 1 84362 016 2
1 3 5 7 9 10 8 6 4 2
Printed in Great Britain

Ruby
the Red
Fairy

by Daisy Meadows

illustrated by Georgie Ripper

ORCHARD BOOKS

The Fairyland Palace

Maze

Forest

Orchard

Black Pot

Meadow

Tower

Beach

Rockpools

Rainspell Island

Shells

Jack Frost's
Ice Castle

Tom Goodfellow's
House

Merry-go-round

Willow
Tree

Mrs Merry's
Cottage

Stream

Field

Town

Mermaid
Cottage

Harbour

Dolphin Cottage

Cold winds blow and thick ice form,
I conjure up this fairy storm.
To seven corners of the mortal world
the Rainbow Fairies will be hurled!

I curse every part of Fairyland,
with a frosty wave of my icy hand.
For now and always, from this fateful day,
Fairyland will be cold and grey!

Contents

The End of the Rainbow

"Look, Dad!" said Rachel Walker. She pointed across the blue-green sea at the rocky island ahead of them. The ferry was sailing towards it, dipping up and down on the rolling waves. "Is that Rainspell Island?" she asked.

Her dad nodded. "Yes, it is," he said, smiling. "Our holiday is about to begin!"

The waves slapped against the side
of the ferry as it bobbed up and down
on the water. Rachel felt her heart
thump with excitement. She could see
white cliffs and emerald green fields on
the island. And golden sandy beaches,
with rock pools dotted here and there.

Suddenly, a few fat raindrops
plopped down on to Rachel's head.
"Oh!" she gasped, surprised. The sun
was still shining.

Rachel's mum grabbed her hand.
"Let's get under cover," she said,
leading Rachel inside.

"Isn't that strange?" Rachel said.
"Sunshine *and* rain!"

"Let's hope the rain stops before we
get off the ferry," said Mr Walker.
"Now, where did I put that map of
the island?"

Rachel looked out of the
window. Her eyes
opened wide.

A girl was standing
alone on the deck.
Her dark hair was
wet with raindrops,
but she didn't seem
to care. She just
stared up at the sky.

Rachel looked over at her mum and dad. They were busy studying the map. So Rachel slipped back outside to see what was so interesting.

And there it was.

In the blue sky, high above them, was the most amazing rainbow that Rachel had ever seen. One end of the rainbow was far out to sea. The other seemed to fall somewhere on Rainspell Island. All of the colours were bright and clear.

Red,
orange,
yellow,
green,
blue,
indigo
and violet.

"Isn't it perfect?" the dark-haired girl whispered to Rachel.

"Yes, it is," Rachel agreed. "Are you going to Rainspell on holiday?"

The girl nodded. "We're staying for a week," she said. "I'm Kirsty Tate."

Rachel smiled, as the rain began to stop. "I'm Rachel Walker. We're staying at Mermaid Cottage," she added.

"And we're at Dolphin Cottage," said Kirsty. "Do you think we might be near each other?"

"I hope so," Rachel replied. She had a feeling she was going to like Kirsty.

Kirsty leaned over the rail and looked down into the shimmering water. "The sea looks really deep, doesn't it?" she said. "There might even be mermaids down there, watching us right now!"

Rachel stared at the waves. She saw something that made her heart skip a beat. "Look!" she said. "Is that a mermaid's hair?" Then she laughed, when she saw that it was just seaweed.

"It could be a mermaid's necklace," said Kirsty, smiling. "Maybe she lost it when she was trying to escape from a sea monster."

The ferry was now sailing into Rainspell's tiny harbour. Seagulls flew around them, and fishing boats bobbed on the water.

"Look at that big white cliff over there," Kirsty said. She pointed it out to Rachel. "It looks a bit like a giant's face, doesn't it?"

Rachel looked, and nodded. Kirsty seemed to see magic *everywhere*.

"There you are, Rachel!" called Mrs Walker. Rachel turned round and saw her mum and dad coming out on to the deck. "We'll be getting off the ferry in a few minutes," Mrs Walker added.

"Mum, Dad, this is Kirsty," Rachel said. "She's staying at Dolphin Cottage."

"That's right next door to ours," said Mr Walker. "I remember seeing it on the map."

Rachel and Kirsty looked at each other in delight.

"I'd better go and find *my* mum and dad," said Kirsty. She looked round. "Oh, here they are."

Kirsty's mum and dad came over
to say hello to the Walkers. Then the
ferry docked, and everyone began to
leave the boat.

"Our cottages are on the other side
of the harbour," said Rachel's dad,
looking at the map. "It's not far."

Mermaid Cottage and Dolphin
Cottage were right next to the beach.
Rachel loved her bedroom, which was
high up, in the attic. From the
window, she could see the waves
rolling onto the sand.

A shout from outside made her look down. It was Kirsty. She was standing under the window, waving at her.

"Let's go and explore the beach!" Kirsty called.

Rachel dashed outside to join her.

Seaweed lay in piles on the sand, and there were tiny pink and white shells dotted about.

"I love it here already!" Rachel shouted happily above the noise of the seagulls.

"Me too," Kirsty said. She pointed up at the sky. "Look, the rainbow's still there."

Rachel looked up. The rainbow glowed brightly among the fluffy white clouds.

"Have you heard the story about the pot of gold at the end of the rainbow?" Kirsty asked.

Rachel nodded. "Yes, but that's just in fairy stories," she said.

Kirsty grinned. "Maybe. But let's go and find out for ourselves!"

"OK," Rachel agreed. "We can explore the island at the same time."

They rushed back to tell their parents where they were going. Then Kirsty and Rachel set off along a lane behind the cottages. It led them away from the beach, across green fields, and towards a small wood.

Rachel kept looking up at the rainbow. She was worried that it would start to fade now that the rain had stopped. But the colours stayed clear and bright.

"It looks like the end of the rainbow is over there," Kirsty said. "Come on!" And she hurried towards the trees.

The wood was cool and green after the heat of the sun. Rachel and Kirsty followed a winding path until they came to a clearing. Then they both stopped and stared.

The rainbow shone down on to the grass through a gap in the trees.

And there, at the rainbow's end, lay an old, black pot.

A Tiny Surprise

"Look!" Kirsty whispered. "There really
is a pot of gold!"

"It could just be a cooking pot,"
Rachel said doubtfully. "Some campers
might have left it behind."

But Kirsty shook her head. "I
don't think so," she said. "It looks
really old."

Rachel stared at the pot. It was sitting on the grass, upside down.

"Let's have a closer look," said Kirsty. She ran to the pot and tried to turn it over. "Oh, it's heavy!" she gasped. She tried again, but the pot didn't move.

Rachel rushed to help her. They both pushed and pushed at the pot. This time it moved, just a little.

"Let's try again," Kirsty panted. "Are you ready, Rachel?"

Tap! Tap! Tap!

Rachel and Kirsty stared at each other.

"What was that?" Rachel gasped.

"I don't know," whispered Kirsty.

Tap! Tap!

"There it is again," Kirsty said. She looked down at the pot lying on the grass. "You know what? I think it's coming from inside this pot!"

Rachel's eyes opened wide. "Are you sure?" She bent down, and put her ear to the pot. *Tap! Tap!* Then, to her amazement, Rachel heard a tiny voice.

"Help!" it called. "Help me!"

Rachel grabbed Kirsty's arm. "Did you hear that?" she asked.

Kirsty nodded. "Quick!" she said. "We *must* turn the pot over!"

Rachel and Kirsty pushed at the pot as hard as they could. It began to rock from side to side on the grass.

"We're nearly there!" Rachel panted. "Keep pushing, Kirsty!"

The girls pushed with all their might. Suddenly, the pot turned over and rolled on to its side. Rachel and Kirsty were taken by surprise. They both lost their balance and landed on the grass with a thump.

"Look!" Kirsty whispered, breathing hard.

A small shower of sparkling red dust had flown out of the pot. Rachel and Kirsty gasped with surprise. The dust hung in the air above them. And there, right in the middle of the glittering cloud, was a tiny winged girl.

28

Rachel and Kirsty watched in wonder as the tiny girl fluttered in the sunlight, her delicate wings sparkling with all the colours of the rainbow.

"Oh, Rachel!" Kirsty whispered. "It's a fairy..."

Fairy Magic

The fairy flew over Rachel and Kirsty's heads. Her short, silky dress was the colour of ripe strawberries. Red crystal earrings glowed in her ears. Her golden hair was plaited with tiny red roses, and her little feet wore crimson slippers.

She waved her scarlet wand, and the shower of sparkling red fairy dust floated softly down to the ground. Where it landed, all sorts of red flowers appeared with a *pop!*

Rachel and Kirsty watched open-mouthed. It really and truly *was* a fairy.

"This is like a dream," Rachel said.

"I always believed in fairies," Kirsty whispered back. "But I never thought I'd ever *see* one!"

The fairy flew towards them. "Oh, thank you *so* much!" she called in a tiny, silvery voice. "I'm free at last!" She glided down, and landed on Kirsty's hand.

Kirsty gasped. The fairy felt lighter and softer than a butterfly.

"I was beginning to think I'd *never* get out of the pot!" the fairy said.

Kirsty wanted to ask the fairy so many things. But she didn't know where to start.

"Tell me your names, quickly," said the fairy. She fluttered up into the air again. "There's so much to be done, and we must get started right away."

Rachel wondered what the fairy meant. "I'm Rachel," she said.

"And I'm Kirsty," said Kirsty. "But who are *you?*"

"I'm the Red Rainbow Fairy – but call me Ruby," the fairy replied.

"Ruby..." Kirsty breathed. "A Rainbow Fairy..." She and Rachel stared at each other in excitement. This really *was* magic!

"Yes," said Ruby. "And I have six sisters: Amber, Saffron, Fern, Sky, Inky and Heather. One for each colour of the rainbow, you see."

"What do Rainbow Fairies do?"
Rachel asked.

Ruby flew over and landed lightly on
Rachel's hand. "It's our job to put all the
different colours into Fairyland," she
explained.

"So why were you shut up inside
that old pot?" asked Rachel.

"And where are your sisters?" Kirsty
added.

Ruby's golden wings drooped. Her
eyes filled with tiny, sparkling tears.
"I don't know," she said. "Something
terrible has happened in Fairyland. We
really need your help!"

Fairies in Danger

Kirsty stared down at Ruby, sitting sadly on Rachel's hand. "Of course we'll help you!" she said.

"Just tell us how," added Rachel.

Ruby wiped the tears from her eyes. "Thank you!" she said. "But first I must show you the terrible thing that has happened. Follow me – as quickly as

you can!" She flew into the air, her
wings shimmering in the
sunshine.

Rachel and Kirsty
followed Ruby across the
clearing. She danced
ahead of them,
glowing like a
crimson flame. She
stopped at a small
pond under a
weeping willow tree.
"Look! I can show
you what happened
yesterday," she said.

She flew over the
pond and scattered another
shower of sparkling fairy dust
with her tiny, red wand. At once,

the water lit up with a strange,
silver light. It bubbled and
fizzed, and then became still.
With wide eyes, Rachel
and Kirsty watched as
a picture appeared.
It was like looking
through a window
into another land!
"Oh, Rachel,
look!" said Kirsty.
A river of
brightest blue ran
swiftly past hills of
greenest green. Scattered
on the hillsides were red
and white toadstool houses.
And on top of the highest hill stood a
silver palace with four pink towers.

The towers were so high, their points were almost hidden by the fluffy white clouds floating past.

Hundreds of fairies were making their way towards the palace. Some were walking and some were flying. Rachel and Kirsty could see goblins, elves, imps and pixies too. Everyone seemed very excited.

"Yesterday was the day of the Fairyland Midsummer Ball," Ruby explained. She flew over the pond and pointed down with her wand to a spot in the middle of the scene. "There I am, with my Rainbow sisters."

Kirsty and Rachel looked closely at where Ruby was pointing. They saw seven fairies, each dressed prettily in their own rainbow colour. Wherever they flew, they left a trail of fairy dust behind them.

"The Midsummer Ball is *very* special," Ruby went on. "And my sisters and I are always in charge of sending out invitations."

To the sound of tinkling music, the front doors of the palace slowly opened.

"Here come King Oberon and Queen Titania," said Ruby. "The Fairy King and Queen. They are about to begin the ball."

Kirsty and Rachel watched as the King and Queen stepped out. The King wore a splendid golden coat and golden crown. His queen wore a silver dress and a tiara that sparkled with diamonds. Everyone cheered loudly. After a while, the King signalled for quiet. "Fairies," he began. "We are very glad to see you all here. Welcome to the Midsummer Ball!"

The fairies clapped their hands and cheered again. A band of green frogs in smart purple outfits started to play, and the dancing began.

Suddenly, a grey mist seemed to fill the room. Kirsty and Rachel watched in alarm as all the fairies started to shiver. And a loud, chilly voice shouted out, "Stop the music!"

The band fell silent. Everyone looked scared. A tall, bony figure was pushing his way through the crowd. He was dressed all in white, and there was frost on his white hair and beard. Icicles hung from his clothes. But his face was red and angry.

"Who's that?" Rachel asked with a shiver. Ice had begun to form around the edge of the pond.

"It's Jack Frost," said Ruby. And she shivered too.

Jack Frost glared at the seven Rainbow Fairies. "Why wasn't I invited to the Midsummer Ball?" he asked coldly.

The Rainbow Fairies gasped in horror...

Ruby looked up from the pond picture. She smiled sadly at Rachel and Kirsty. "Yes, we forgot to invite Jack Frost," she said.

The Fairy Queen stepped forward. "You are very welcome, Jack Frost," she said. "Please stay and enjoy the ball."

But Jack Frost looked even more angry. "Too late!" he hissed. "You forgot to invite me!" He turned and pointed a thin, icy finger at the Rainbow Fairies.

"Well, you will not forget this!" he went on. "My spell will banish the Rainbow Fairies to the seven corners of the mortal world. From this day on, Fairyland will be without colour — for ever!"

Jack Frost's Spell

As Jack Frost cast his spell, a great, icy wind began to blow. It picked up the seven Rainbow Fairies and spun them up into the darkening sky. The other fairies watched in dismay.

Jack Frost turned to the King and Queen. "Your Rainbow Fairies will be trapped, never to return." With that, he left, leaving a trail of icy footprints.

Quickly, the Fairy Queen stepped forward and lifted her silver wand. "I cannot undo Jack Frost's magic completely," she shouted, as the wind howled and rushed around her. "But I can guide the Rainbow Fairies to a safe place until they can be rescued!"

The Queen pointed her wand at the

grey sky overhead. A black pot came
spinning through the stormy clouds. It
flew towards the Rainbow Fairies. One
by one, the Rainbow Fairies tumbled
into the pot.

"Pot-at-the-end-of-the-rainbow, keep
our Rainbow Fairies safely together,"
the Queen called. "And take them to
Rainspell Island!"

The pot flew out of sight, behind a dark cloud. And the bright colours of Fairyland began to fade, until it looked like an old black and white photograph.

"Oh no!" Kirsty gasped. Then the picture in the pond vanished.

"So the Fairy Queen cast her *own* spell!" Rachel said. She was bursting with questions. "She put you and your sisters in the pot, and sent you to Rainspell."

Ruby nodded. "Our Queen knew that we would be safe here," she said. "We know Rainspell well. It is a place full of magic."

"But where are your sisters?" Kirsty wanted to know. "They were in the pot too."

Ruby looked upset. "Jack Frost's spell must have been stronger than the Queen thought," she said. "As the pot spun through the sky, the wind blew my sisters out again. I was at the bottom, so I was safe. But I was trapped when the pot landed upside down."

"So are your sisters somewhere on Rainspell?" Kirsty asked.

Ruby nodded. "Yes, but they're scattered all over the island. Jack Frost's spell has trapped them too." She flew towards Kirsty and landed on her shoulder. "That's where you and Rachel come in."

"How?" Rachel asked.

"You found *me*, didn't you?" the fairy went on. "That's because you believe in magic." She flew from Kirsty's shoulder to Rachel's. "So, you could rescue my Rainbow sisters too! Then we can all bring colour back to Fairyland again."

"Of course we'll search for your sisters,"
Kirsty said quickly. "Won't we,
Rachel?"

Rachel nodded.

"Oh, thank you," Ruby said happily.

"But we're only here for a week,"
Rachel said. "Will that be long enough?"

"We must get started right away,"

said Ruby. "First, I must take you to Fairyland to meet our King and Queen. They will be very pleased to know that you are going to help me find my sisters."

Rachel and Kirsty stared at Ruby.

"You're taking us to *Fairyland?*" Kirsty gasped. She could hardly believe her ears. Nor could Rachel.

"But how will we get there?" Rachel wanted to know.

"We'll fly there," Ruby replied.

"But *we* can't fly!" Rachel pointed out.

Ruby smiled. She whirled up into the air and flew over the girls' heads. Then she swirled her wand above them. Magic red fairy dust fluttered down.

Rachel and Kirsty began to feel a bit
strange. Were the trees
getting bigger or were
they getting smaller?

They were getting smaller!
Smaller and smaller and
smaller, until they were
the same size as Ruby.

"I'm tiny!" Rachel laughed.
She was so small, the flowers around
her seemed like trees.

Kirsty twisted round to look at her
back. She had wings –
shiny and delicate
as a butterfly's!
Ruby beamed
at them. "Now
you can fly,"
she said. "Let's go."

Rachel twitched her shoulders. Her
wings fluttered, and she felt herself rise up
into the air. She felt quite wobbly at first.
It was very odd!

"Help!" Kirsty yelled, as she shot up
into the air. "I'm not very good at this!"

"Come on," said Ruby, taking their hands. "I'll help you." She led them up, out of the glade.

Rachel looked down on Rainspell Island. She could see the cottages next to the beach, and the harbour.

"Where *is* Fairyland, Ruby?" Kirsty asked. They were flying higher and higher, up into the clouds.

"It's so far away, that no mortal could ever find it," Ruby said.

They flew on through the clouds for a long, long time. But at last Ruby turned to them and smiled. "We're here," she said.

As they flew down from the clouds, Kirsty and Rachel saw places they recognised from the pond picture: the palace, the hillsides with their toadstool houses, the river and flowers. But there were no bright colours now. Because of Jack Frost's spell, everything was a drab shade of grey. Even the air felt cold and damp.

A few fairies walked miserably across
the hillsides. Their wings hung limply
down their backs. No one could
be bothered to fly.

Suddenly, one of the fairies looked up
into the sky. "Look!" she shouted. "It's
Ruby. She's come back!"

At once, the fairies flew up towards Ruby, Kirsty and Rachel. They circled around them, looking much happier, and asking lots of questions.

"Have you come from Rainspell, Ruby?"

"Where are the other Rainbow Fairies?"

"Who are your friends?"

"First, we must see the King and Queen. Then I will tell you everything!" Ruby promised.

King Oberon and Queen Titania were seated on their thrones. Their palace was as grey and gloomy as everywhere else in Fairyland. But they smiled warmly when Ruby arrived with Rachel and Kirsty.

"Welcome back, Ruby," the Queen said. "We have missed you."

"Your Majesties, I have found two mortals who believe in magic!" Ruby announced. "These are my friends, Kirsty and Rachel."

Quickly Ruby explained what had happened to the other Rainbow Fairies. She told everyone how Rachel and Kirsty had rescued her.

"You have our thanks," the King told them. "Our Rainbow Fairies are very special to us."

"And will you help us to find Ruby's Rainbow sisters?" the Queen asked.

"Yes, we will," Kirsty said.

"But how will we know where to look?" Rachel wanted to know.

"The trick is not to look too hard," said Queen Titania. "Don't worry. As you enjoy the rest of your holiday, the magic you need to find each Rainbow Fairy will find *you*. Just wait and see."

King Oberon rubbed his beard thoughtfully. "You have six days of your holiday left, and six fairies to find," he said. "A fairy each day. That's a lot of fairy-finding. You will need some special help." He nodded at one of his footmen, a plump frog in a buttoned-up jacket.

The frog hopped over to Rachel and Kirsty and handed them each a tiny, silver bag.

"The bags contain magic tools," the Queen told them. "Don't look inside them yet. Open them only when you really need to, and you will find something to help you." She smiled at Kirsty and Rachel.

"Look!" shouted another frog footman suddenly. "Ruby is beginning to fade!"

Rachel and Kirsty looked at Ruby in horror. The fairy was growing paler before their eyes. Her lovely dress was no longer red but pink, and her golden hair was turning white.

"Jack Frost's magic is still at work," said the King, looking worried. "We cannot undo his spell until the Rainbow Fairies are all together again."

"Quickly, Ruby!" urged the Queen. "You must return to Rainspell at once."

Ruby, Kirsty and Rachel rose into the air, their wings fluttering.

"Don't worry!" Kirsty called, as they flew higher. "We'll be back with all the Rainbow Fairies very soon!"

"Good luck!" called the King and Queen.

Rachel and Kirsty watched Ruby worriedly as they flew off. But as they got further away from Fairyland, Ruby's colour began to return. Soon she was bright and sparkling again.

They reached Rainspell at last. Ruby led Rachel and Kirsty to the clearing in the wood, and they landed next to the old, black pot. Then Ruby scattered fairy dust over Rachel and Kirsty. There was a puff of glittering red smoke, and the two girls shot up to their normal size again. Rachel wriggled her shoulders. Yes, her wings had gone. "Oh, I really *loved* being a fairy," Kirsty said. They watched as Ruby sprinkled her magic dust over the old, black pot.

"What are you doing?" Rachel asked.

"Jack Frost's magic means that I can't help you look for my sisters," Ruby replied sadly. "So I will wait for you here, in the pot-at-the-end-of-the-rainbow."

Suddenly the pot began to move. It rolled across the grass, and stopped under the weeping willow tree. The tree's branches hung right down to the ground.

"The pot will be hidden under the tree," Ruby explained. "I'll be safe there."

"We'd better start looking for the other Rainbow Fairies," Rachel said to Kirsty. "Where shall we start?"

Ruby shook her head. "Remember what the Queen said," she told them. "The magic will come to you." She flew over and sat on the edge of the pot. Then she pushed aside one of the willow branches and waved at Rachel and Kirsty. "Goodbye, and good luck!"

"We'll be back soon, Ruby," Kirsty promised.

"We're going to find all your Rainbow sisters," Rachel said firmly. "Just you wait and see!"

RAINBOW magic

Ruby is safely hidden in the
pot-at-the-end-of-the-rainbow.
Now Rachel and Kirsty must find
Amber the Orange Fairy

A Very Unusual Shell

"What a lovely day!" Rachel Walker shouted, staring up at the blue sky. She and her friend, Kirsty Tate, were running along Rainspell Island's yellow, sandy beach. Their parents walked a little way behind them.

"It's a *magical* day," Kirsty added. The two friends smiled at each other.

Rachel and Kirsty had come to Rainspell Island for their holidays. They had soon found out it really *was* a magical place!

As they ran, they passed rock pools that shone like jewels in the sunshine.

Rachel spotted a little *splash!* in one of the pools. "There's something in there, Kirsty!" she pointed. "Let's go and look."

The girls jogged over to the pool and crouched down to see.

Kirsty's heart thumped as she gazed into the crystal clear water. "What is it?" she asked.

Suddenly, the water rippled. A little brown crab scuttled sideways across the sandy bottom and vanished under a rock.

Kirsty felt disappointed. "I thought it might be another Rainbow Fairy," she said.

"So did I, "Rachel sighed. "Never mind. We'll keep on looking."

"Of course we will," Kirsty agreed. Then she put her finger to her lips as their parents came up behind them. "*Ssh*."

Kirsty and Rachel had a big secret. They were helping to find the Rainbow Fairies. Thanks to Jack Frost's wicked spell, the fairies were lost on Rainspell Island. And until they were all found there would be no colour in Fairyland.

Rachel looked at the shimmering blue sea. "Shall we have a swim?" she asked.

But Kirsty wasn't listening. She was
shading her eyes with her hand and
looking further along the beach. "Over
there, Rachel – by those rocks," she
said.

Then Rachel could see it too –
something winking and sparkling in the
sunshine. "Wait for me!" she called, as
Kirsty hurried over there.

When they saw what it was, the two
friends sighed in disappointment.

"It's just the wrapper from a
chocolate bar," Rachel said sadly. She
bent down and picked up the shiny
purple foil.

Kirsty thought for a moment. "Do
you remember what the Fairy Queen
said?" she asked.

Rachel nodded. "*Let the magic come to*

you," she said. "You're right, Kirsty.
We should just enjoy our holiday, and
wait for the magic to happen."

Read the rest of

Amber the Orange Fairy

to find out what magic
happens next...

RAINBOW magic

by Daisy Meadows

Ruby the Red Fairy   ISBN   1 84362 016 2
She's all alone on Rainspell Island...until Rachel and Kirsty promise to track down her Rainbow sisters.

Amber the Orange Fairy   ISBN   1 84362 017 0
She's trapped tight in an unusual place. Can a fluffy feather help rescue her?

Saffron the Yellow Fairy   ISBN   1 84362 018 9
She's stuck in a very sticky situation. How will Rachel and Kirsty free her?

Fern the Green Fairy   ISBN   1 84362 019 7
She's lost in a leafy hollow. And there's a secret to solve to save her.

Sky the Blue Fairy   ISBN   1 84362 020 0
She's having some bubble trouble. Can the rainbow-coloured crab help?

Inky the Indigo Fairy   ISBN   1 84362 021 9
She's up to her usual mischief. Rachel and Kirsty must get her back to the pot...before it's too late.

Heather the Violet Fairy   ISBN   1 84362 022 7
She's in a spin. Until the colourful carousel horses rush to her rescue.

All priced at £3.99
Rainbow Magic books are available from all good bookshops,
or can be ordered direct from the publisher:
Orchard Books, PO BOX 29, Douglas IM99 1BQ
Credit card orders please telephone 01624 836000
or fax 01624 837033 or visit our Internet site: www.wattspub.co.uk
or e-mail: bookshop@enterprise.net for details.

To order please quote title, author and ISBN
and your full name and address.
Cheques and postal orders should be made payable to 'Bookpost plc.'
Postage and packing is FREE within the UK
(overseas customers should add £1.00 per book).

Prices and availability are subject to change.